AmaZing ~Animal
~~ AlphaRhymes ~~

Advanced

More Animal Facts
For Older Children

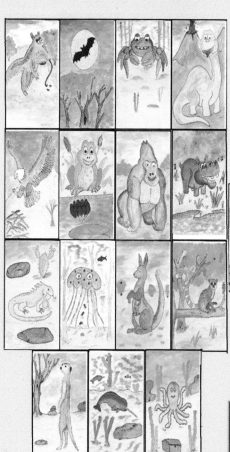

AmaZing~Animal ~~ AlphaRhymes ~~

by Sandra Stoner-Mitchell

A is for Anteater
he has a great big nose,
his tongue is long and sticky
and it reaches to his toes.
He pokes it into anthills,
and the ants cannot pull free,
and when he pulls it out
again,
he eats them for his tea.

Facts on Anteaters

Giant Anteaters hunt for food at night and sleep nearly 15 hours a day. They do not have teeth so they use their long, sticky tongues which can reach up to two feet in length to catch the insects to eat.

Anteaters have a very strong sense of smell, about 40 times that of humans. Their claws are very sharp and strong, enough to open concrete-hard termite and ant mounds.

Although they eat about 30,000 insects a day, Anteaters only stay a few minutes at a termite or ant mound, taking only a few thousand insects from each nest.

B is for the bat
in the dark they are not blind,
they have the use of sonar
when their food they're off to
find.
While most bats feed on
insects,
a group like fruit to eat,
but there are some who sup
on blood.
Perhaps it tastes quite sweet!

Facts on Bats

A small Bat can eat up to 1000 mosquitoes in just one hour. They are also the longest-lived mammal for its size with a life span of almost forty years.

Some Bats now have a highly sophisticated sense of hearing. Bats emit sounds that bounce off objects in their path, which then sends echoes back to them. From these echoes the Bats can determine the size of objects, how far away they are, how fast they are travelling and even their texture, all in a split second.

Bats find shelter in caves, crevices, tree cavities and buildings. Some species are solitary while others form colonies of more than a million individuals.

In the UK, Bats are a protected species.

C is for the Crab,
they like pinching people's
toes,
and if you put your face too
close
they'll even pinch your nose.
Crabs like eating algae
it's a green and slimy mess,
so if you ask them round for
lunch,
you'll know what they like
best.

Facts on Crabs

Crabs have 10 legs, but the first pair are called claws. They also have a thick external skeleton which helps protect the soft tissue underneath. Crabs live in all the world's oceans, in fresh water and on land. There are over 4,500 species. Crabs usually have a distinct sideways walk. However, some Crabs can walk forwards or backwards, and some are capable of swimming.

A group of Crabs are called a cast. They can communicate with each other by drumming or waving their pincers. Crabs eat both meat and plants but they feed mainly on algae and bacteria, other crustaceans, molluscs, worms, and fungi.

Some Crab species can get rid of limbs such as their claws and grow them back again later. Male Crabs tend to often fight each other over females or hiding holes.

D is for the Dinosaur,
they were very big,
you wouldn't want to meet
one,
he would snap you like a twig.
Some liked eating vegetables,
and the others liked their
meat.
Thank goodness they have
gone now,
or it could be us they'd eat!

Facts on Dinosaurs

Dinosaurs ruled the Earth for over 160 million years. It is believed that Dinosaurs lived on Earth until around 65 million years ago when a mass extinction occurred. Scientists believe that the event leading to the extinction may have been a massive asteroid impact or huge volcanic activity. Events such as these could have blocked out sunlight and significantly changed the Earth's environment. Rather than being meat eaters, the largest Dinosaurs were actually plant eaters. To help fight meat eaters many plant eaters had natural weapons at their disposal such as spikes on the tail or three horns attached to the front of their head shield.

E is for the Eagle
they fly high up in the sky.
They can see the smallest
creature
as they go flying by.
They like catching mice to eat,
and will catch them as they
run.
They like chasing rabbits too,
and sometimes just for fun.

Facts on Eagles

Eagles have very unusual eyes with a million light-sensitive cells which means they have five times more than us humans. While we see three basic colours Eagles see five. These differences give the Eagle really good eyesight and even the most well camouflaged prey are not safe from them. It is believed an Eagle can spot an animal the size of a rabbit up to two miles away.

Some Eagles have only short wings but have long tails which allows them to hunt in the tight confines of the forests. Others have a very wide wingspan allowing them to soar high in the sky over plains and water.

In Greece, the Golden Eagle eats turtles, flying up high with them in their strong claws, they can then drop them onto the rocks to smash their very tough shells.

F is for the frog
he's a crafty little thing,
he sits down very quietly
his tongue coiled like a spring.
Then when a fly comes whizzing
by
the frog's tongue zooms out
fast,
the fly is stuck, the frog is
pleased,
his dinner's there at last!

Facts on Frogs

Frogs lay their eggs in water, which then hatch into tadpoles. The tadpoles then live in water until they change into adult Frogs.

Tadpoles look more like fish than Frogs, they have long finned tails and breathe through gills just like a fish. Although Frogs live on land their habitat must be near water, this is because they will die if their skin dries out. Frogs use their sticky, strong tongue to catch and swallow food. Unlike us their tongue is not attached to the back of its mouth, instead it is attached to the front, enabling the Frog to stick its tongue out much further.

Frogs can see forwards, sideways and upwards all at the same time and they never close their eyes, even when they sleep.

Another strange thing about Frogs is they actually use their eyes to help them swallow food. When the Frog blinks its eyeballs are pushed downwards creating a bulge in the roof of its mouth. This bulge squeezes the food inside the Frog's mouth down the back of its throat. This is especially helpful for the breed of Frogs that have no tongues.

G is for Gorilla,
they look so mean and tough,
they stand up tall and are so
strong,
but they're not really gruff.
They like to eat bamboo and
leaves,
then look through their
mate's hair
to pick out juicy nits and
bugs,
they know they'll find in there.

Facts on Gorillas

Gorillas are endangered animals, their habitat is being destroyed by people who are using the land which gorillas live in for farming and the trees for firewood. Gorillas are known to be some of the strongest and most intelligent animals in the world and live in the wild for an average of 35 years.

Mountain Gorillas live in groups with many females and their offspring, while the lowland Gorilla lives in smaller family groups. Both groups are led by a dominant male who will defend his group, even to the death.

Gorillas have 98% human DNA and have unique finger prints, the same as humans.

Gorilla children are very similar in behaviour to human children, enjoying their first few years chasing and playing with each other and climbing trees.

H is for the Hippo,
he has a great big head,
and a monstrous mouth and
body
which he likes to keep well
fed.
I don't know how he got so
big
he mostly eats the grass,
but even though he weighs a
lot
he can run very fast.

Facts on Hippos

Hippopotamus sunbathe on the shoreline and give out an oily red substance that people once believed to be blood. The liquid is actually a skin moistener and sun block which is also thought to provide protection against germs.

When they are underwater Hippos need to surface every 3 to 5 minutes to breathe. They do this automatically and even when sleeping under water they will rise and breathe without waking.

Each female has one calf every two years. Soon after birth mother and calf with join schools that provide some protection from crocodiles, lions and hyenas.

I is for Iguana,
their tails are very long
they use them when they're threatened,
like a whip because they're strong.
They swim and run and climb up trees,
but they don't make a noise.
They eat their meals of fruit and greens,
just like young girls and boys.

Facts on Iguanas

Iguanas mainly eat aubergines, leaves and fruit, they will also eat small insects. They have very sharp teeth to help them eat the leaves and plants but they will also use them with their sharp claws and long tails to attack if they feel threatened.

Iguanas have spines along their backs to help protect them against their enemies. They also have lots of extra skin below their necks called a dewlap. This helps them to control their body temperature, which is helpful as they are cold-blooded and their bodies don't control their body temperatures automatically.

Iguanas have a third eye on the top of their head. This eye isn't quite like the normal eye, but it helps Iguana's sense movement from their enemies sneaking up behind them.

The Green Iguana can fall 40 – 50 feet and survive which is handy if they fall from a tree!

J is for the Jellyfish,
and although some look pretty,
they are not a friendly bunch
they sting which is a pity.
They eat small plants and tiny
fish,
but don't have brains or heart,
and jellyfish don't have
backbones;
you'd think they'd fall apart!

Facts on Jellyfish

Some Jellyfish are bigger than a human and others are as small as a pinhead! In some parts of the world millions of Jellyfish will swarm together, they are called a 'Bloom'. These blooms can cause lots of problems for fishermen and tourism. Some Jellyfish have millions of tiny stinging cells in their tentacles, they are used to capture food.

Jellyfish are very important in the ocean, we should not harm them, they are food for many marine animals such as large fish and turtles. They are also good for providing somewhere for the many tiny fish to hide and also protect them from being eaten by larger fish.

Many young Crabs hitchhike on the top of a Jellyfish so they don't have to swim.

K is for the Kangaroo,
the red ones have big feet,
they hop faster than horses
run,
and they can swim a treat.
The babies are called Joeys,
and you'll never hear them
grouch
when mum jumps up and
bounces,
while they're safe inside her
pouch.

Facts on Kangaroos

Kangaroos are found in Australia and Tasmania and live in forests and on grassy plains. They live in organised groups led by the largest male.

The male Kangaroo is called a Boomer, Buck or Jack. Females are called Does, Flyers, or Jills and the young ones are called Joeys.

The female Kangaroo usually have one Joey at a time and the newborn only weighs 0.03 ounces at birth, as small as a little bean! After birth, Joey has a long crawl into its mother's pouch and it will stay there until it has grown and is properly developed. Red Kangaroo Joeys do not leave their mothers pouch until they are 8 months old. The Grey Kangaroo Joeys wait until they are almost a year old.

L is for the Lemur,
they have the longest tails.
They make the strangest
noises,
with their snorts and clicks
and wails.
The ring-tailed Lemur's are so
clean
when stroked, you'll hear
them purr.
They eat bananas, figs and
leaves,
then sit and comb their fur.

Facts on Lemurs

Grooming themselves and being with their family members is an important part of the Lemur's life. In the first two weeks of a newborns life it will be carried around in its mother's mouth, then when the baby is strong enough it will hold on to her back to be carried around.

The two ways the Lemurs have of communicating with each other is by various sounds and scent markings. They are able to identify family members by the scent they release.

There are many stories about the Lemurs in Roman Mythology, some say the Lemur is an evil spirit and should be avoided, others say they are good luck.

M is for the Meerkat,
their colour helps them hide,
they burrow tunnels
underground
with lots of rooms each side.
They hunt for birds and lizards,
some fruit and insects too,
to share it with their family
and friends just like we do.

Facts on Meerkats

Just like humans the Meerkat can recognise the different sounds of members from their clan.

Meerkat hunt together looking for food. While some members are hunting others have the job of lookout, if an enemy comes close they send out a series of cries to warn the rest of their clan.

Another thing Meerkat do is 'babysit' any pups while the elders are away hunting. This job generally goes to one male or female, a young adult, or whoever is the least hungry. The 'sitter' is usually rewarded with food at the end of the day.

Adult Meerkat teach their young how to hunt. Although Meercats are immune to a Scorpion's poison they can still do a lot of damage to them with their sharp pinchers.

The Meerkat clans are usually about 40 or 50 members, all are related to the dominant pair, but it is the female who rules them all.

N is for the Narwhal,
which means, one-tooth-one-horn.
They are quite white when they are old,
grey-blue when they are born.
They eat the fish from arctic water,
so cold from the North Pole.
They have no teeth but that's okay
they swallow their food whole.

Facts on Narwhals

The Narwhal is called the Unicorn of the sea. Their long spiral tusk is one of two teeth, the long one growing through the top lip, up to the size of 8ft 8ins (2.7 meters) long. The females sometimes grow their own tusk but it is very small. The Narwhal travel in groups and are often seen swimming in groups of 15 -20 but they have been seen in gatherings of hundreds and even thousands. The larger groups have sometimes been trapped by shifting ice and then become victim to Polar Bears, or Walruses.

They feed on fish, Shrimp, Squid, and other aquatic life.

O is for the Octopus,
their blood is coloured blue.
They have three hearts, they
don't have bones,
they're very clever, too.
They have hard beaks; their
tongues have teeth,
they're masters of disguise.
If arms drop off, they'll grow
again,
Well, that was a surprise!

Facts on Octopuses

The Octopus's tentacles are actually called arms and it is now said that two of them are legs as they have been observed using the same two to push themselves off the seabed.

The Octopus has an amazing ability to change its colour in just three tenths of a second, not only that they can change their appearance to blend in with the rocks and plants around itself. Sharks, Eels and Dolphins will swim past without seeing it.

If an Octopus is caught it lets out a jet of blue venom giving it the chance to get away, if that isn't enough, it can 'lose' an arm and grow it back later.

Octopuses don't live very long, only a few years, some die within months. They are very intelligent and some scientists believe if the Octopus lived longer, they would be the dominant intelligence of all living species, including us!

P is for the Porcupine,
their quills are sharp and long.
Their sight is poor, but that's
all right,
their sense of smell is strong.
They eat a lot of different trees
and also shrubby bark,
and some can see the
porcupine
in woodlands after dark.

Facts on Porcupines

Porcupines can vary in size from 1 inch to 40 inches with their weight varying between 1kg to 27kg.

They feed on many types of trees and dandelions, pondweeds, water lilies and clover. Their favourite flavour is salt and they have been seen eating the hose on car radiators. Porcupines have 20 teeth and live for about 20 years. Their quills lie flat on their backs but when a predator attacks, they spike up in defence. They have about 30,000 quills on their bodies. When they shake their body some quills will fall off, these are collected and worn by many African tribes as ornaments. They believe the quills will bring them good luck. The hollow quills are sometimes used as musical instruments.

Q is for the Quail,
they make grass nests on the
ground,
they have a plume upon their
head
that bobs as they walk round.
They sometimes make a high
pitched squeal,
but screech and grunt to talk,
and as they can't fly very far
they mostly have to walk.

Facts on Quail

Most Quails are decorated with stripes, bars or spots which help them to blend in with their surroundings and avoid drawing attention to themselves.

Although Quail can fly, they have spent so much time on the ground that they are happier walking and fly only if they feel threatened.

Young Quail mature quickly and can usually feed themselves within a few days of hatching.

Quail have a varied diet of plant and animal foods, they also eat insects and fruit as part of their staple diet.

R is for the Reindeer,
they live where it is cold,
to keep them warm they have two
coats,
to save the heat they hold.
To find the moss, the food they
love,
in places they may go,
their sense of smell is strong
enough
to find it under snow.

Facts on Reindeer

Both the male and female Reindeer have antlers, the female keeps hers through the winter until they give birth to their young in the spring. Male reindeer shed their antlers at the start of winter and grow them again in spring the following year.

Their sense of smell is so strong they can find food as deep as 60 centimetres under the snow.

There are certain types of lichen that grow in sub-arctic climate that help keep their blood warm so they can survive the icy cold winters.

When the weather falls below freezing Reindeer have the ability to lower the temperature in their legs to near freezing levels to keep the rest of their body heat at an even temperature, aiding their survival.

S is for the Spider,
most have four sets of eyes,
they spin their webs of sticky
silk
to capture bugs and flies.
Spider mums are very good,
they watch their young with
care.
They're also good for gardens,
as they catch the bugs out
there.

Facts on Spiders

The Spider's silk is the strongest material in the world. Scientists have not been able to recreate this design even with all the technology we have today.

The Spider's blood is a light blue colour.

The stickiness of a Spider web makes it very hard to keep dust out, this is why they are always remaking them.

When a Spider is going to make a new web it will roll up it's old cobweb up and inject it with their venom, which then turns it into a liquid substance that they can drink. They do the same to the bugs and flies that are trapped in their web. That is the only way they can eat.

The male spider is often smaller than the female who can deliver up to 3000 eggs at a time.

T is for the Turtle,
sixty bones make up their
shells.
They lay their eggs beneath
the sand,
but can't walk very well.
Their front flippers help them
to swim,
their back ones help them
steer.
They lose salt water through
their eyes
which look like tiny tears.

Facts on Turtles

60 different bones are connected to make Turtles hard shells.

Leatherback Turtles are the longest at six and a half feet long (1.8m).

Turtles can live between 40 and over 100 years.

The 7 species of Turtles we have in our seas now have been around for over 110 million years!

They can stay under the water for as long as five hours at a time.

A Turtles heart rate slows down to preserve oxygen when underwater and nine minutes can elapse between each heartbeat.

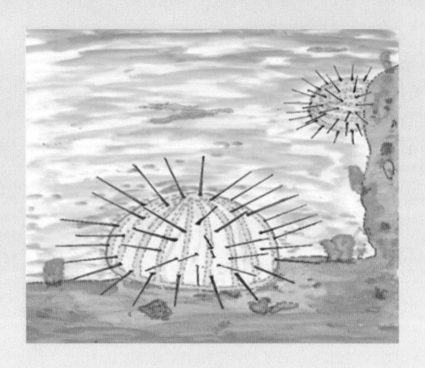

U is for the Urchin.
They look cute, but don't go
near,
their needles can be painful
so it's wise to stay well clear.
Their mouth is underneath,
so when they search the
ocean floor,
the urchins are prepared to
eat
the food they're searching for.

Facts on Urchins

There are over 200 species of Sea Urchins and they come in many colours from sandy yellows to bright pinks and dark purples. They have five sections that are exactly the same size.

Some Urchins have poisonous soft spines.

They have five sets of 'legs' that are really tubes they use to propel themselves across the ocean floor.

Urchins live in warm water oceans and can live up to 200 years, but most only live for 30.

They do not have faces as such, but they do have a mouth and an anus. Their simple digestive system means they can easily get rid of what they don't need.

Urchins mainly eat algae and other easily digestible vegetation. Their mouth is at the bottom half of their body and they scurry around on their 'legs' eating whatever they come across on the ocean floor.

V is for the Vulture
that no one understands,
they clean up all the mess
around,
creating healthy lands.
They don't harm other
creatures,
they prefer to fly away
and they are sick around their
nests,
to keep predators at bay!

Facts on the Vulture

It is the Day of the Vulture on the first Saturday of September every year to try and raise awareness of this much-maligned creature. Nothing goes to waste with a Vulture, they clean up the land making it a much healthier place. Vultures even make good use of semi-digested food, they will regurgitate it around their nest site because they have learned that the stench is off-putting to predators, therefore keeping their eggs safe. Vultures will also regurgitate food to get away from an enemy quickly, it makes them lighter and gives them a better chance to fly off.

W is the Walrus
they have brown deep
wrinkled skin,
covering mounds of blubber
keeping cold out when they
swim.
They snort and bellow when
they talk,
their long tusks break the ice,
their favourite food is shellfish
and they think clams are
really nice.

Facts on Walruses

Walruses are the gentle giants of the Arctic. They are among the largest pinnipeds - fin-footed, semi aquatic marine mammals.

However, while they have an intimidating size, and are carnivores, these animals are not aggressive.

The Walrus' favourite food is shellfish. They dive underwater and use their whiskers to detect the shellfish in the dark waters of the ocean.

Walruses have large, flabby bodies covered in brown or pink skin. Short fur covers most of their bodies except for their fins. Their faces feature two small eyes, a moustache and two long tusks.

Some research has estimated the Walrus will eat up to 4,000 clams in one feeding! They detect shellfish by using their sensitive whiskers in the dark waters of the ocean.

As soon as a Walrus is born it can swim and stays with its mother for the first three years.

X is for X-ray-Tetra,
fish, with skeletons on show.
Their silver, pastel-yellow fins
send out a twinkling glow.
They feed on worms and insects
living on the river bed.
Their babies aren't called X-
Rays,
we have called them Fry
instead.

Facts on X-Ray-Tetra

X-Ray Tetra fish have a bone structure which is known as the Weberian apparatus, named after Max Webber, in which the structure is used to pick up sound waves and brings about an acute sense of hearing.

X-ray Tetra mainly hunt worms, insects and small crustaceans that live close to the river bed.

The transparency of their skin is thought to be a form of protection as predators find it much harder to spot them amongst dense vegetation and shimmering water.

The biggest threat to the X-Ray-Tetra is water pollution.

Y is for the Yak
they have long, thick, furry hair,
they live high in the mountains
in the freezing cold thin air.
Their horns are so enormous,
they are needed when they
fight,
and Yaks enjoy a lovely bath,
Iced water is just right.

Facts on Yaks

There are two types of Yak, the Wild Yak and the Domestic Yak. The Domestic Yak is smaller and its coat is less furry.

Yaks have long, upward curled horns that are located on the each side of the head. Horns in males are twice as long as in females and they can reach 40 inches in length.

The Yak can survive in the Himalayas at an altitude as high as 20,000 feet, they are able to survive such high altitudes because they have large lungs so they can inhale lots of oxygen.

The Yaks digestive system allows them to digest at a temperature of 104 degrees Fahrenheit keeping it warm even in the extreme cold conditions.

Z is for the Zebra,
they are sociable and smart,
they like to group together,
when they talk they snort and
bark.
While sleeping they stay
standing up,
and some remain on guard.
The muddle of their stripes will
then
make catching them quite hard.

Facts on Zebra

Zebra sleep standing up but only if they are with a group of Zebras. While they sleep, there are always others around keeping guard against attack, not only from other animals but from humans too.

Hunters kill them for their skin. They have a language for talking to each other through braying, barking and whinnying. They also have facial expressions to show their disapproval, their ears go flat on their heads, when that happens it is warning to keep your distance.

Zebras have black and white striped coats that are unique to each one.

Other books by Sandra
Stoner-Mitchell

Hedgerow Capers Series:

Hedgerow Capers
The Day Before Christmas Eve
The Fun Begins
A Spot of Bother

~~

Casper the Caterpillar
The Witch and the Fairy

Sandra Stoner-Mitchell was born in Ipswich, Suffolk but spent most of her life in the South of England. She lived in Spain for several years with her husband, learning the language and writing but recently they moved back to the South of England.

Sandra began writing stories and poems at an early age but has only started having her work published in the last couple of years.

You can find out more about Sandra and her books on her website and Facebook. You can also follow her on Twitter:

http://sandrascapers.com

https://www.facebook.com/hedgerowvillagecapers

https://twitter.com/hedgerowcapers

You can find all of Sandra's books on Amazon:

U.S. *http://www.amazon.com/Sandra-Stoner-Mitchell/e/B009UZFOGG*
U.K. *http://www.amazon.co.uk/Sandra-Stoner-Mitchell/e/B009UZFOGG*